Ready-to-Read

# Mitchell Is Moving

By Marjorie Weinman Sharmat

Pictures by
Jose Aruego & Ariane Dewey

COLLIER BOOKS

Macmillan Publishing Company
New York
Collier Macmillan Publishers
London

Text copyright © 1978 by Marjorie Weinman Sharmat
Illustrations copyright © 1978 by Jose Aruego and Ariane Dewey
All rights reserved. No part of this book may be reproduced or transmitted
in any form or by any means, electronic or mechanical, including
photocopying, recording or by any information storage and retrieval system,
without permission in writing from the Publisher.
Macmillan Publishing Company, 866 Third Avenue, New York, N.Y. 10022
Collier Macmillan Canada, Inc.
*Mitchell Is Moving* is also published in a hardcover edition by Macmillan Publishing Company.
First Collier Books edition 1985
Printed in the United States of America
10  9  8  7  6  5  4  3  2  1
LIBRARY OF CONGRESS CATALOGING IN PUBLICATION DATA
Sharmat, Marjorie Weinman.   Mitchell is moving.   (Ready-to-Read)
SUMMARY: A dinosaur's exuberance about moving cools considerably
when he realizes how much he misses his next-door friend.
[1. Moving, Household—Fiction.   2. Friendship—Fiction.   3. Dinosaurs—Fiction]
I. Aruego, Jose.   II. Dewey, Ariane.   III. Title.
PZ7.S5299Mi    [E]    85-47782   ISBN 0-02-045260-8

*For Mitchell
and our good move of February 24th
with love*

Mitchell ran through his house.
"So long. So long, everything,"
he shouted.

Then he ran next door
to Margo's house.
"I'm moving," he said.
"Where?" asked Margo.
"Two weeks away," said Mitchell.
"Where is that?" asked Margo.

"It's wherever I will be
after I walk for two weeks,"
said Mitchell. "I have lived
in the same place
for a long time.
It is time for me
to go someplace else."

"No!" said Margo. "You have only
lived next door
for fifty years."
"Sixty," said Mitchell.
"Fifty, sixty. What's the difference?"
said Margo. "I want you to stay
next door forever."

"I can't," said Mitchell.
"I do not want to wake up
in the same old bedroom
and eat breakfast
in the same old kitchen
and brush my scales
and clean my nails
in the same old bathroom.
Every room in my house
is the same old room
because I have been there
too long."

"Well, maybe you are just tired
of the same old friend," said Margo.
"Who is that?" asked Mitchell.
"Me," said Margo.
"Maybe you look at me
and think,
   'Same Old Face.
   Same Old Tail.
   Same Old Scales.
   Same Old Walk.
   Same Old Talk.
   Same Old Margo.'"

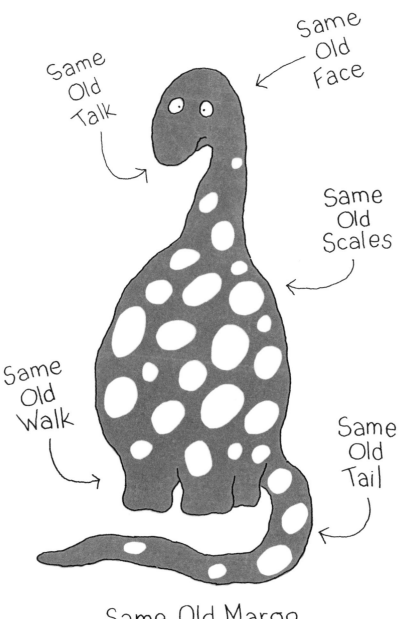

Same Old Margo

"No," said Mitchell.

"I like your face, tail,
    scales, walk and talk.
    I like you."

"I like, like, like you,"
    said Margo.

"I like, like, like you, too,"
    said Mitchell.

He walked to the door.

"I must pack," he said.

Margo sat down

in front of the door.

"You can't get out,"

she said. "I will sit here

for another sixty years."

"I still like you!" shouted Mitchell

as he climbed out the window.

Margo called after him,
"I will glue you to your roof.
I will tie you
to your front door
with a thick green rope.
I will scotch-tape you,
paper-clip you to your house.
Then I will get
a gigantic rubber band
and loop you to your house.
I will not let you leave."

"I will unglue, untie, untape,
unclip and unloop myself,"
said Mitchell.
Mitchell ran around his house.
"I'm moving, moving, moving,"
he shouted.

Then he gathered up
some of the slimy moss near his house
and wrapped it in silver foil.
"Just in case there is no slimy moss
two weeks away."

18

Mitchell scooped up some mud
from a ditch.
"Maybe there is no mud
two weeks away.
Or no swamp water," he said
as he filled a plastic bag
with water from his swamp
and mud from his ditch.

Mitchell went into his house
and put the slimy moss
and mud and swamp water
into his suitcase.

The telephone rang.
Mitchell answered it.
"I will cement you
    to your ceiling," said Margo,
and she hung up.

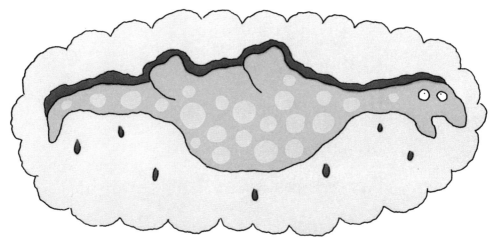

"I am beginning to think
that Margo does not want
me to move," said Mitchell
as he went back
to his packing.
He packed the
cap and mitten set
that Margo had given him.
"Maybe it will be cold
two weeks away," he thought.

Mitchell heard a shout.
He went to his window.
Margo was shouting,
"I will take you
to the laundromat
in my laundry bag,
and I will wash away
your idea of moving."
"Margo is a good shouter,"
thought Mitchell.

He remembered when
Margo had sent him
a Happy Birthday Shout
through the window:
"I'M GLAD YOU'RE THERE.
I'M GLAD I'M HERE.
HAPPY BIRTHDAY,
LOUD AND CLEAR."

"I wonder if there are any
Happy Birthday Shouters
two weeks away,"
thought Mitchell.

Mitchell held up the T-shirt
that Margo had given him.
It said,
MITCHELL, FRIEND OF MARGO
MARGO, FRIEND OF MITCHELL
"This shirt makes me feel sad
that I am moving," said Mitchell.
"But if I put it on
I won't have to look at it."
Mitchell put on the T-shirt.
"If I don't look down
at my chest,
I will feel all right."

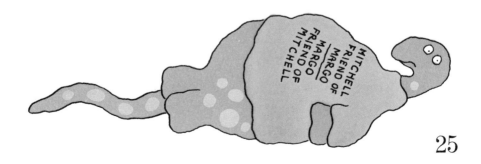

25

He closed his suitcase.

"There. I am all packed.

I am ready to go."

Mitchell walked through his house.

"So long, same old rooms," he said.

Mitchell took his suitcase

and went to Margo's house.

"I am all ready

to move," he said.

"I will stick you
    to your house
    with chewing gum,"
    said Margo.
    Mitchell picked up his suitcase
    and ran.
"Good-by!" he called.
"I will write to you
    every day."

Mitchell stopped running
and started to walk fast.
"I am a moving Mitchell,"
he said.
Mitchell walked and walked.

When night came,

he sent Margo a post card that said,

    Dear Margo,

    greetings from

    one day away.

The second night he wrote,

    Dear Margo,

    more greetings from

    two days away.

The third night he wrote,
   Dear Margo,
   more and more greetings
   from three days away.
"I am not much
   of a post-card writer,"
   thought Mitchell.
But he sent more and more
   greetings to Margo
   each night.

At last Mitchell reached
two weeks away.
"I made it!" he said.

Mitchell built a house
and moved in.

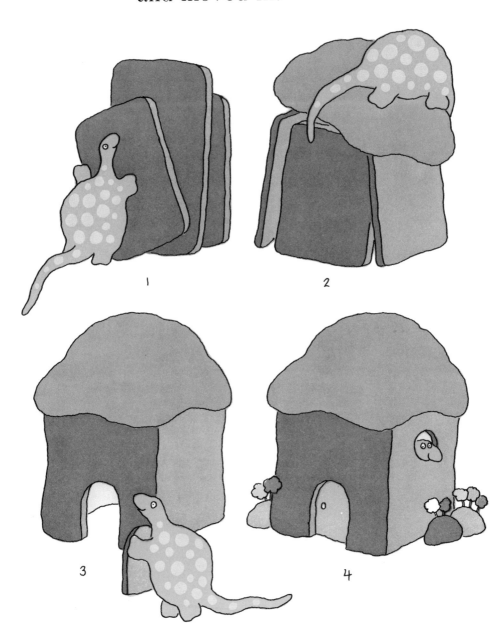

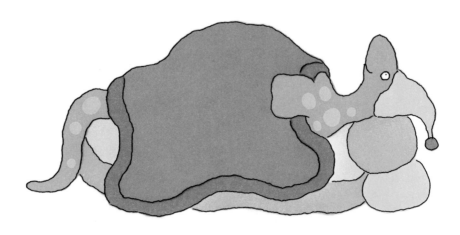

"I will go to bed right away
so I can wake up
in my new bedroom," he said.
"Mmm. New sleeps better,"
Mitchell said the next day.
"Now I will eat my first meal
in my new kitchen.
Mmm. New tastes better."

Mitchell went outside
and sat down in front of his house.
"This is a good house," he said.
"But there is something missing.
There is nobody next door.
What good is a good house
when there is nobody
next door to it?
I am lonely.
I miss Margo."

Mitchell wrote a post card to Margo:

Dear Margo,

the most greetings ever

from two weeks away.

The slimy moss is nice and slimy.

The mud is nice and thick.

The swamp water

is nice and mucky.

But I miss you.

Please come to see me.

Mitchell waited and waited.

And waited.

One morning he woke up

and saw a bottle of glue,

a thick green rope,

a big roll of Scotch tape,

a huge paper clip,

a gigantic rubber band,

a laundry bag,

a sack of cement

and a package of chewing gum.

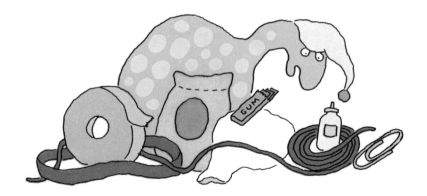

Then he saw Margo.

"Mitchell!" said Margo.

"Margo!" said Mitchell.

"I am so happy to see you.

Here is my new house
and my new everything."
Mitchell showed Margo
his new house
and everything around it.

"Two weeks away is terrific,"
said Margo as she and Mitchell
ate breakfast.
"No, it isn't," said Mitchell.

"There is nobody next door."

"Oh," said Margo.

"I have the same problem
  where I am.
    There is nobody next door."

"I have an idea," said Mitchell,
   and he got some twigs and mud.
"I have the same idea," said Margo,
   and she filled her laundry bag
   with more twigs and mud.

Then she got her bottle of glue,

thick green rope,

big roll of Scotch tape,

huge paper clip,

gigantic rubber band

and sack of cement.

"We can use these, too,"

she said.

Mitchell and Margo built a house
next door to Mitchell's house.

"Do you like it?" asked Mitchell.

"It's perfect," said Margo.

Margo moved into her new house.

She shouted,

"I'VE COME TO STAY

TWO WEEKS AWAY.

HAPPY BIRTHDAY."

It wasn't Mitchell's birthday.

But he was happy anyway.

MARJORIE WEINMAN SHARMAT's inimitable blend of humor and sensitivity has made her books popular with youngsters of all ages. Her other Ready-to-Read books include *Griselda's New Year* and *Sophie and Gussie*. For the picture-book age, she has written *Gila Monsters Meet You at the Airport* (also a Reading Rainbow selection), *Bartholomew the Bossy*, *The 329th Friend* and many other books, and her older fans have enjoyed such books as *51 Sycamore Lane* (paperback edition titled *The Spy in the Neighborhood*).

Ms. Sharmat lives in Tucson, Arizona.

JOSE ARUEGO and ARIANE DEWEY have collaborated on the illustrations for many beautiful children's books, including *The Chick and the Duckling, Mushroom in the Rain, Rum Pum Pum* and *Gregory, the Terrible Eater* (also a Reading Rainbow selection).

Both Mr. Aruego and Ms. Dewey live in New York City.